The New Baby

by Lynne Benton and Rupert Van Wyk

W
FRANKLIN WATTS
LONDON•SYDNEY

"Soon we will have a new baby," said Mum.

"I want a baby sister," said Holly.

"I don't want a baby brother."

"We won't know if it's a baby boy or a baby girl until it's here," said Mum. "We will have to wait and see."

Holly looked at the girls
in the park.

"I want a sister," she said.

"She will play with me."

Then Holly looked at the boys.

"I don't want a brother," she said.

One day Mum said,

"Today our baby will come."

"Oh good," said Holly.

"I hope it will be a baby sister."

"We'll find out soon," said Mum.

"Have a good day at school."

When Holly came home from school,
the new baby was there.
"You have a baby brother, Holly,"
said Mum.

Holly was cross.

"I wanted a sister," she said.

Mum smiled.

"When I was a little girl, my mum had a baby. I wanted a sister too," she said. "But I got a brother."

"Were you cross?" asked Holly.

"No," said Mum. "My baby brother is your Uncle Tim."

Holly smiled.

"I like Uncle Tim," she said.

"He is good fun."

"Yes," said Mum. "I liked having a baby brother. I played games with Uncle Tim and had lots of fun. Maybe your brother will be just like him."

Holly looked at

her new baby brother.

He was very small.

But he would get bigger.

Then they could play together.

Holly put out her finger,

and her brother squeezed tightly.

"He likes me!" said Holly.

"Yes," said Mum.

"You are his big sister.

You will have a lot of fun together."

Holly smiled.

"I'm glad I have a brother," she said.

Story order

Look at these 5 pictures and captions.
Put the pictures in the right order
to retell the story.

1

Holly remembers playing with Uncle Tim.

2

Holly goes off to school for the day.

3

Holly sees some girls in the park.

4

Holly offers the baby her finger.

5

Mum tells Holly she has a new brother.

Independent Reading

This series is designed to provide an opportunity for your child to read on their own. These notes are written for you to help your child choose a book and to read it independently.

In school, your child's teacher will often be using reading books which have been banded to support the process of learning to read. Use the book band colour your child is reading in school to help you make a good choice. *The New Baby* is a good choice for children reading at Orange Band in their classroom to read independently.

The aim of independent reading is to read this book with ease, so that your child enjoys the story and relates it to their own experiences.

About the book

Holly's mum is having a baby. Holly thinks only a sister will be a fun addition to the family. When Holly learns that her awesome Uncle Tim is a little brother to her mum, she realises that brothers are great too!

Before reading

Help your child to learn how to make good choices by asking: "Why did you choose this book? Why do you think you will enjoy it?" Look at the cover together and ask: "What do you think the story will be about?" Ask your child to think of what they already know about the story context. Then ask your child to read the title aloud. Establish that in this book, a new baby arrives.

Ask: "How do you think the little girl feels about the new baby? Why might she be feeling that way?"

Remind your child that they can sound out the letters to make a word if they get stuck.

Decide together whether your child will read the story independently or read it aloud to you.

During reading

Remind your child of what they know and what they can do independently. If reading aloud, support your child if they hesitate or ask for help by telling the word. If reading to themselves, remind your child that they can come and ask for your help if stuck.

After reading

Support comprehension by asking your child to tell you about the story. Use the story order puzzle to encourage your child to retell the story in the right sequence, in their own words. The correct sequence can be found at the bottom of the next page.

Help your child think about the messages in the book that go beyond the story and ask: "What was Holly guessing about little brothers that might not be true? Can you think of some brothers you know that are great fun?"

Give your child a chance to respond to the story: "Did you have a favourite part? Were you pleased when Holly changed her mind about the baby? Why/why not?"

Extending learning

Help your child understand the story structure by using the same sentence patterning and adding different elements. "Let's make up a new story about siblings. How many siblings is your story about? What struggles might they face? How can they learn to get along?"

In the classroom, your child's teacher may be teaching how to read words with contractions. There are many examples in this book that you could look at with your child, for example: *don't, didn't, won't, it's*. Find these together and point out how the apostrophe indicates a missing letter or letters.

Franklin Watts
First published in Great Britain in 2020
by The Watts Publishing Group

Copyright © The Watts Publishing Group 2020

Series Editors: Jackie Hamley, Melanie Palmer and Grace Glendinning
Series Advisors: Dr Sue Bodman and Glen Franklin
Series Designers: Peter Scoulding and Cathryn Gilbert

A CIP catalogue record for this book is
available from the British Library.

ISBN 978 1 4451 7097 8 (hbk)
ISBN 978 1 4451 7099 2 (pbk)
ISBN 978 1 4451 7098 5 (library ebook)

Printed in China

Franklin Watts
An imprint of
Hachette Children's Group
Part of The Watts Publishing Group
Carmelite House
50 Victoria Embankment
London EC4Y 0DZ

An Hachette UK Company
www.hachette.co.uk

www.franklinwatts.co.uk

FSC
www.fsc.org
MIX
Paper from
responsible sources
FSC® C104740

Answer to Story order: 3, 2, 5, 1, 4